Oscar got the blame.

Tony Ross

Dial Books for Young Readers
·New York·

To Katy,
and her invisible friend Mandy,
who made the endpapers of this book
out of a clean piece of paper

First published in the United States 1988 by
Dial Books for Young Readers
A Division of NAL Penguin Inc.
2 Park Avenue
New York, New York 10016

Published simultaneously in Canada by Fitzhenry & Whiteside Limited, Toronto
Originally published in Great Britain by Andersen Press Ltd.
Copyright © 1988 by Tony Ross
All rights reserved
Printed in England by W. S. Cowell Ltd.
First Edition
C O B E
2 4 6 8 10 9 7 5 3 1

Library of Congress Cataloging in Publication Data
Ross, Tony. Oscar got the blame.
Summary: Nobody but Oscar can see Billy,
so when anything bad happens around the house,
it's Oscar who gets the blame.
[1. Behavior—Fiction. 2. Imaginary playmates—Fiction.]
I. Title. PZ7.R71992Os 1988 [E] 87-15543
ISBN 0-8037-0497-6
ISBN 0-8037-0499-2 (lib. bdg.)

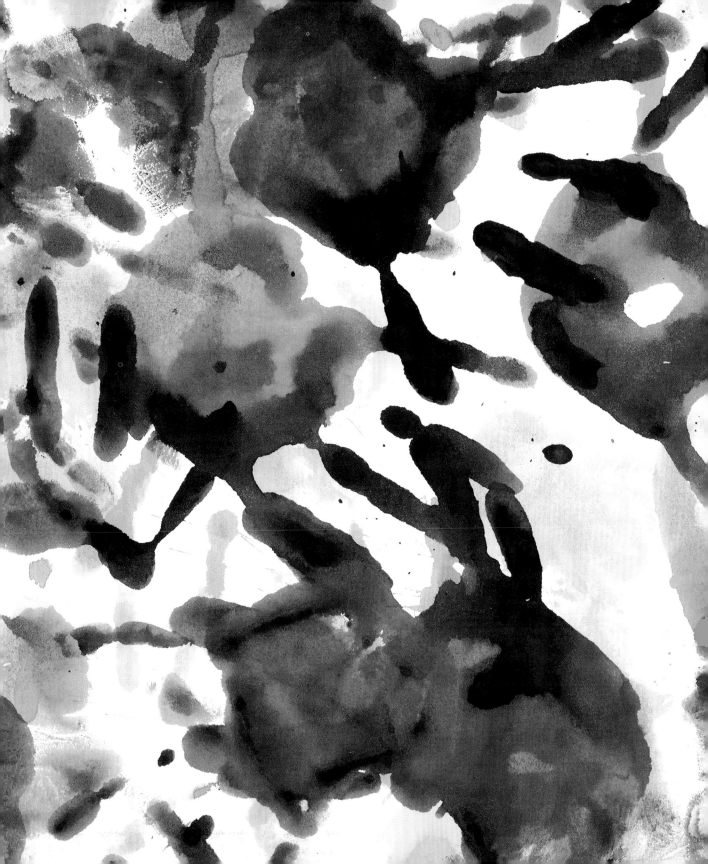

This is Oscar . . .

and this is Oscar's friend, Billy.
Oscar's mom and dad think Oscar made Billy up.

Whenever Oscar talked about Billy, his mom and dad said, "Don't be silly."

But Oscar and Billy were the best of friends . . .

day and night.

Sometimes Oscar let Billy have some of his dinner . . .

but then he had to eat it all himself.

When Billy left little bits of mud around the house . . .

Oscar got the blame.

When Billy dressed the dog in Dad's things . . .

Oscar got the blame.

When Billy put frogs in Granny's slippers...

Oscar got the blame.

When Billy made breakfast . . .

Oscar got the blame.

When Billy washed the cat . . .

Oscar got the blame.

And when Billy left the water running in the bathroom . . .

Oscar got the blame . . .

and he was sent to bed without a story.

"It's not fair!" cried Oscar.
"Nobody believes in my friend Billy."

"THEY NEVER DO!" said Billy.